Lillie THE Lion

Written and illustrated By
Richard Tudor

Ever since she was Small, Lillie Liked to Roar

When she went to her friends, she wouldn't knock the door

She would stand up straight and breathe in deep

Then Roar so loud, they could not sleep

They would roll out of bed and onto the floor

Lillie was here, they could tell by the Roar

Opening the door to see her smiles

She could be heard for miles and miles

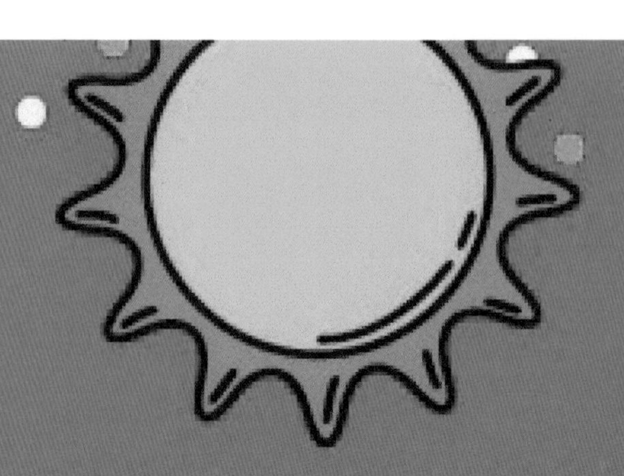

They would laugh and play and have such fun
All day long under the bright bright
sun

Before going home they would ask for one
more

Come on Lillie give us a......

ROOOOOAAAAARRRRR!!!!

The End

Ellis THE Elephant

Written and illustrated By
Richard Tudor

All day long, she likes to trump and play

You will not miss her, she is big and grey

With great big ears and the longest nose

You are sure to see her, wherever she goes

In the jungle, or in the water to dunk

You can still spot her enormous trunk

Playing with friends and hanging around

Her hose for a nose, makes the greatest sound

Her Friends all agree, one of the greatest joys

Is sitting around and hearing that noise

Whenever they're sad or down in the dump

They just ask Ellis to give us a............

TRUUUUUUUUMMMMP!!!

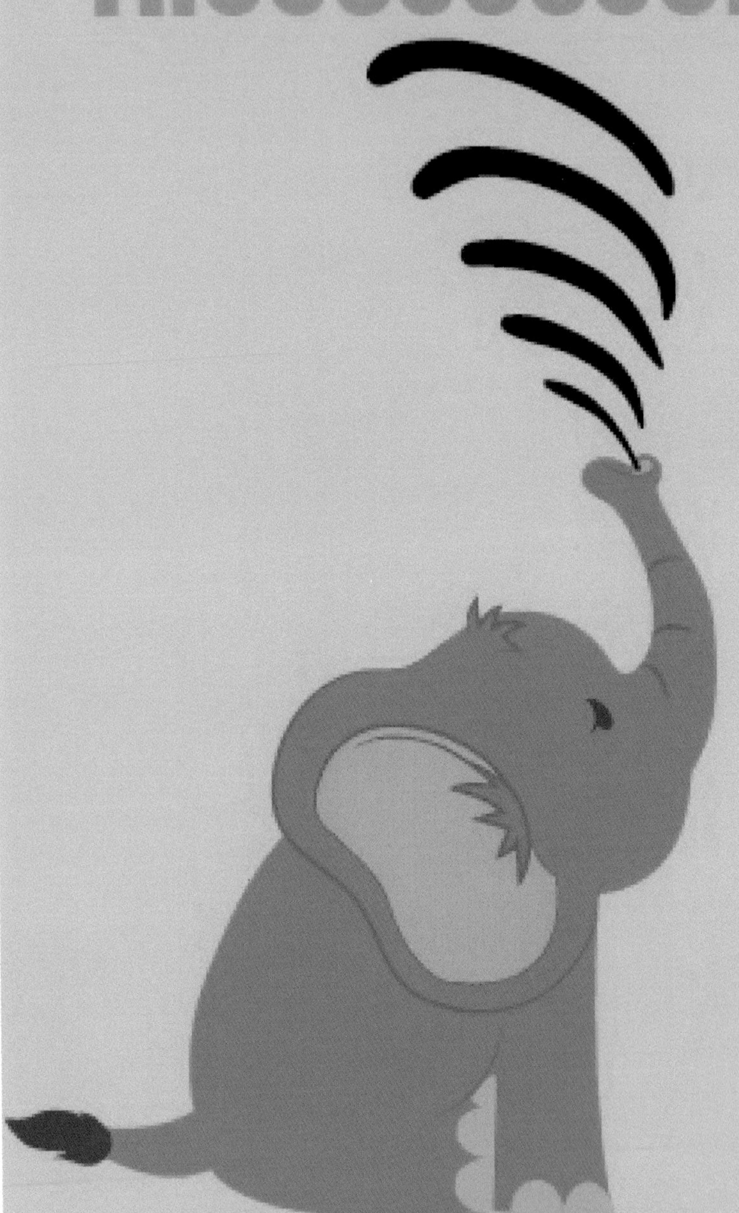

The End

Written and illustrated By
Richard Tudor

Small and fluffy and ever so cute

Kerry is quiet, she won't even toot

If you want to find her, then look to the sky

She isn't a bird, but she climbs ever so high

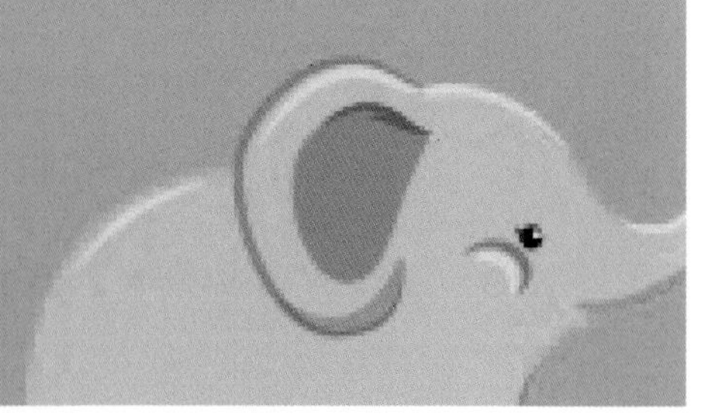

Eating her leaves and sleeping all day

She only wakes up for her friends to play

She sits with them all and keeps them snug

Kerry is the best at giving a hug

Her fur is so soft and smile so wide

Kerry and the others like to seek and hide

When they get lost and seem in a muddle

They just ask Kerry to give us a............

CUDDLE!!!!

The End

Polly THE Panda

Written and illustrated By
Richard Tudor

Black and White with eyes wide and bright

Polly is pretty and a wonderful sight

If you want to find her then all you do

Is search in the grass and around the bamboo

She likes to play and have lots of fun

Sitting and rolling and trying to run

She is just young, so now is just small

But when she grows up she'll be very tall

Polly loves, a stick to twirl

Twizzle and twist or just to hurl

To hear her sneeze, then lucky you

She has the loudest ah, AH..........

ACHOOOOO!!!

The End

Ricky THE Racoon

Written and illustrated By
Richard Tudor

Spending all year to gather his food

Ricky is cheeky and a little bit rude

He often tells, a funny riddle

To make his friends, give a giggle

With rings all around, he has a big bushy tail
Making the day fun, he never does fail

His friends all love him for being funny

They sit and listen, when it's nice and sunny

But if he sees you, when you're having lunch

He will try to swipe some and have a munch

He is a little bit stinky, because he does not bath

But his friends don't mind, Because he makes them...........

LAUGH!!!!!!

The End

Printed in Great Britain
by Amazon